1 MONTH OF
FREE
READING

at

www.ForgottenBooks.com

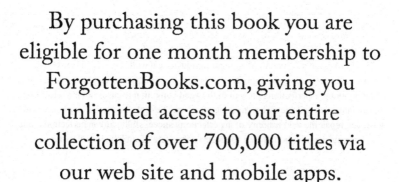

By purchasing this book you are
eligible for one month membership to
ForgottenBooks.com, giving you
unlimited access to our entire
collection of over 700,000 titles via
our web site and mobile apps.

To claim your free month visit:

www.forgottenbooks.com/free283122

ISBN 978-0-267-68643-8
PIBN 10283122

THE

Badminton Magazine

October 1898

SOME EXPERIENCES OF AN IRISH R.M.

BY E. Œ. SOMERVILLE AND MARTIN ROSS

No. I.—GREAT-UNCLE McCARTHY

A RESIDENT Magistracy in Ireland is not an easy thing to come
by nowadays; neither is it a very attractive job; yet on the
evening when I first propounded the idea to the young lady who
had recently consented to become Mrs. Sinclair Yeates, it seemed
glittering with possibilities. There was, on that occasion, a
sunset, and a string band playing 'The Gondoliers,' and there
was also an ingenuous belief in the omnipotence of a godfather
of Philippa's—(Philippa was the young lady)—who had once been
a member of the Government.

I was then climbing the steep ascent of the Captains towards
my Majority. I have no fault to find with Philippa's godfather;
he did all and more than even Philippa had expected; nevertheless,
I had attained to the dignity of mud major, and had spent a good
deal on postage stamps, and on railway fares to interview people
of influence, before I found myself in the hotel at Skebawn,
opening long envelopes addressed to 'Major Yeates, R.M.'

My most immediate concern, as anyone who has spent nine
weeks at Mrs. Raverty's hotel will readily believe, was to leave
it at the earliest opportunity; but in those nine weeks I had
learned, amongst other painful things, a little, a very little, of
the methods of the artizan in the West of Ireland. Finding

a house had been easy enough. I had had my choice of
several, each with some hundreds of acres of shooting, thoroughly
poached, and a considerable portion of the roof intact. I had
selected one; the one that had the largest extent of roof in
proportion to the shooting, and had been assured by my landlord
that in a fortnight or so it would be fit for occupation.

'There's a few little odd things to be done,' he said easily;
' a lick of paint here and there, and a slap of plaster——'

I am short-sighted, I am also of Irish extraction, both facts
that make for toleration, but even I thought he was understat-
ing the case. So did the contractor.

At the end of three weeks the latter reported progress, which
mainly consisted of the facts that the plumber had accused the
carpenter of stealing sixteen feet of his inch-pipe to run a bell
wire through, and that the carpenter had replied that he wished
the divil might run the plumber through a wran's quill. The
plumber, having reflected upon the carpenter's parentage, the
work of renovation had merged in battle, and at the next Petty
Sessions I was reluctantly compelled to allot to each combatant
seven days, without the option of a fine.

These and kindred difficulties extended in an unbroken chain
through the summer months, until a certain wet and windy day
in October, when, with my baggage, I drove over to establish
myself at Shreelane. It was a tall, ugly house of three stories
high, its walls faced with weather-beaten slates, its windows
staring, narrow, and vacant. Round the house ran an area, in
which grew some laurustinus and holly bushes among ash heaps,
and nettles, and broken bottles. I stood on the steps, waiting
for the door to be opened, while the rain sluiced upon me from a
broken eaveshoot that had, amongst many other things, escaped
the notice of my landlord. I thought of Philippa, and of her
plan, broached in to-day's letter, of having the hall done up as a
sitting-room.

The door opened, and revealed the hall. It struck me that
I had perhaps overestimated its possibilities. Among them I
had certainly not included a flagged floor, sweating with damp,
and a reek of cabbage from the adjacent kitchen stairs. A large
elderly woman, with a red face, and a cap worn helmet-wise on
her forehead, swept me a magnificent curtsey as I crossed the
threshold.

'Your honour's welcome——' she began, and then every door
in the house slammed in obedience to the gust that drove through
it. With something that sounded like ' Mend ye for a back door!'

Mrs. Cadogan abandoned her opening speech and made for the kitchen stairs. (Improbable as it may appear, my housekeeper was called Cadogan, a name made locally possible by being pronounced Caydogawn.)

Only those who have been through a similar experience can know what manner of afternoon I spent. I am a martyr to colds in the head, and I felt one coming on. I made a laager in front of the dining-room fire, with a tattered leather screen and the dinner table, and gradually, with cigarettes and strong tea, baffled the smell of must and cats, and fervently trusted

I STOOD ON THE STEPS, WAITING FOR THE DOOR TO BE OPENED

that the rain might avert a threatened visit from my landlord. I was then but superficially acquainted with Mr. Florence McCarthy Knox and his habits.

At about 4.30, when the room had warmed up, and my cold was yielding to treatment, Mrs. Cadogan entered and informed me that 'Mr. Flurry' was in the yard, and would be thankful if I'd go out to him, for he couldn't come in. Many are the privileges of the female sex; had I been a woman I should unhesitatingly have said that I had a cold in my head. Being a man, I huddled on a mackintosh, and went out into the yard.

My landlord was there on horseback, and with him there was a man standing at the head of a stout grey animal. I recognised with despair that I was about to be compelled to buy a horse.

'Good afternoon, Major,' said Mr. Knox in his slow, sing-song brogue; 'it's rather soon to be paying you a visit, but I thought you might be in a hurry to see the horse I was telling you of.'

I could have laughed. As if I were ever in a hurry to see a horse. I thanked him, and suggested that it was rather wet for horse-dealing.

'Oh, it's nothing when you're used to it,' replied Mr. Knox. His gloveless hands were red and wet, the rain ran down his nose, and his covert coat was soaked to a sodden brown. I thought that I did not want to become used to it. My relations with horses have been of a purely military character. I have endured the Sandhurst riding school, I have galloped for an impetuous general, I have been steward at regimental races, but none of these feats has altered my opinion that the horse, as a means of locomotion, is obsolete. Nevertheless, the man who accepts a resident magistracy in the south-west of Ireland voluntarily retires into the prehistoric age; to institute a stable became inevitable.

'You ought to throw a leg over him,' said Mr. Knox, 'and you're welcome to take him over a fence or two if you like. He's a nice flippant jumper.'

Even to my unexacting eye the grey horse did not seem to promise flippancy, nor did I at all desire to find that quality in him. I explained that I wanted something to drive, and not to ride.

'Well, that's a fine raking horse in harness,' said Mr. Knox, looking at me with his serious grey eyes, 'and you'd drive him with a sop of hay in his mouth. Bring him up here, Michael.'

Michael abandoned his efforts to kick the grey horse's forelegs into a becoming position, and led him up to me.

I regarded him from under my umbrella with a quite unreasonable disfavour. He had the dreadful beauty of a horse in a toyshop, as chubby, as wooden, and as conscientiously dappled, but it was unreasonable to urge this as an objection, and I was incapable of finding any more technical drawback. Yielding to circumstance, I 'threw my leg' over the brute, and after pacing gravely round the quadrangle that formed the yard, and jolting to my entrance gate and back, I decided that as he had neither fallen down nor kicked me off, it was worth paying twenty-five pounds for him, if only to get in out of the rain.

MICHAEL ABANDONED HIS EFFORTS TO KICK THE GREY HORSE'S FORELEGS
INTO A BECOMING POSITION

Mr. Knox accompanied me into the house and had a drink. He was a fair, spare young man, who looked like a stable boy among gentlemen, and a gentleman among stable boys. He belonged to a clan that cropped up in every grade of society in the county, from Sir Valentine Knox of Castle Knox down to the auctioneer Knox, who bore the attractive title of Larry the Liar. So far as I could judge, Florence McCarthy of that ilk occupied a shifting position about midway in the tribe. I had met him at dinner at Sir Valentine's, I had heard of him at an illicit auction, held by Larry the Liar, of rum stolen from a wreck. They were 'Black Protestants,' all of them, in virtue of their descent from a godly soldier of Cromwell, and all were prepared at any moment of the day or night to sell a horse.

' You'll be apt to find this place a bit lonesome after the hotel,' remarked Mr. Flurry, sympathetically, as he placed his foot in its steaming boot on the hob, ' but it's a fine sound house any- way, and lots of rooms in it, though indeed, to tell you the truth, I never was through the whole of them since the time my great- uncle, Denis McCarthy, died here. The dear knows I had enough of it that time.' He paused, and lit a cigarette—one of my best, and quite thrown away upon him. ' Those top floors, now,' he resumed, ' I wouldn't make too free with them. There's some of them would jump under you like a spring bed. Many's the night I was in and out of those attics, following my poor uncle when he had the bad turn on him—the horrors, y' know— there were nights he never stopped walking through the house. Good Lord! will I ever forget the morning he said he saw the devil coming up the avenue ! " Look at the two horns on him," says he, and he out with his gun and shot him, and, begad, it was his own donkey ! '

Mr. Knox gave a couple of short laughs. He seldom laughed, having in unusual perfection the gravity of manner that is bred by horse-dealing, probably from the habitual repression of all emotion save disparagement.

The autumn evening, grey with rain, was darkening in the tall windows, and the wind was beginning to make bullying rushes among the shrubs in the area ; a shower of soot rattled down the chimney and fell on the hearthrug.

' More rain coming,' said Mr. Knox, rising composedly : ' you'll have to put a goose down these chimneys some day soon, it's the only way in the world to clean them. Well, I'm for the road. You'll come out on the grey next week, I hope ; the hounds'll be meeting here. Give a roar at him coming in at his jumps.' He threw his cigarette into the fire and extended a hand to me. 'Good-bye, Major, you'll see plenty of me and my hounds before you're done. There's a power of foxes in the plantations here.'

This was scarcely reassuring for a man who hoped to shoot woodcock, and I hinted as much.

'Oh, is it the cock?' said Mr. Flurry; 'b'leeve me, there never was a woodcock yet that minded hounds, now, no more than they'd mind rabbits! The best shoots ever I had here, the hounds were in it the day before.'

When Mr. Knox had gone, I began to picture myself going across country roaring, like a man on a fire engine, while Philippa put the goose down the chimney; but when I sat down to write to her I did not feel equal to being humorous about it. I dilated ponderously on my cold, my hard work, and my loneliness, and eventually went to bed at ten o'clock full of cold shivers and hot whisky-and-water.

After a couple of hours of feverish dozing, I began to understand what had driven Great-Uncle McCarthy to perambulate the house by night. Mrs. Cadogan had assured me that the Pope of Rome hadn't a betther bed undher him than myself; wasn't I down on the new flog mattherass the old masther bought in Father Scanlan's auction? By the smell I recognised that 'flog' meant flock, otherwise I should have said my couch was stuffed with old boots. I have seldom spent a more wretched night. The rain drummed with soft fingers on my window panes; the house was full of noises. I seemed to see Great-Uncle McCarthy ranging the passages with Flurry at his heels; several times I thought I heard him. Whisperings seemed borne on the wind through my keyhole, boards creaked in the room overhead, and once I could have sworn that a hand passed, groping, over the panels of my door. I am, I may admit, a believer in ghosts; I even take in a paper that deals with their culture, but I cannot pretend that on that night I looked forward to a manifestation of Great-Uncle McCarthy with any enthusiasm.

The morning broke stormily, and I woke to find Mrs. Cadogan's understudy, a grimy nephew of about eighteen, standing by my bedside, with a black bottle in his hand.

'There's no bath in the house, sir,' was his reply to my command; 'but me A'nt said, would ye like a taggeen?'

This alternative proved to be a glass of raw whisky. I declined it.

I look back to that first week of housekeeping at Shreelane

as to a comedy excessively badly staged, and striped with lurid melodrama. Towards its close I was positively home-sick for Mrs. Raverty's, and I had not a single clean pair of boots. I am not one of those who hold the convention that in Ireland the rain never ceases, day or night, but I must say that my first November at Shreclane was composed of weather of which my friend Flurry Knox remarked that you wouldn't meet a Christian out of doors, unless it was a snipe or a dispensary doctor. To this lamentable category might be added a resident magistrate. Daily, shrouded in mackintosh, I set forth for the Petty Sessions Courts of my wide district; daily, in the inevitable atmosphere of wet frieze and perjury, I listened to indictments of old women who plucked geese alive, of publicans whose hospitality to their friends broke forth uncontrollably on Sunday afternoons, of 'parties' who, in the language of the police sergeant, were subtly defined as 'not to say dhrunk, but in good fighting thrim.'

I got used to it all in time—I suppose one can get used to anything—I even became callous to the surprises of Mrs. Cadogan's cooking. As the weather hardened and the woodcock came in, and one by one I discovered and nailed up the rat holes, I began to find life endurable, and even to feel some remote sensation of home coming when the grey horse turned in at the gate of Shreelane.

The one feature of my establishment to which I could not become inured was the pervading sub-presence of some thing or things which, for my own convenience, I summarised as Great-Uncle McCarthy. There were nights on which I was certain that I heard the inebriate shuffle of his foot overhead, the touch of his fumbling hand against the walls. There were dark times before the dawn when sounds went to and fro, the moving of weights, the creaking of doors, a far-away rapping in which was a workmanlike suggestion of the undertaker, a rumble of wheels on the avenue. Once I was impelled to the perhaps imprudent measure of cross-examining Mrs. Cadogan. Mrs. Cadogan, taking the preliminary precaution of crossing herself, asked me fatefully what day of the week it was.

'Friday!' she repeated after me. 'Friday! The Lord save us! 'Twas a Friday the old masther was buried.'

At this point a saucepan opportunely boiled over, and Mrs. Cadogan fled with it to the scullery, and was seen no more.

In the process of time I brought Great-Uncle McCarthy down to a fine point. On Friday nights he made coffins and drove hearses, during the rest of the week he rarely did more than patter and shuffle in the attics over my head.

One night, about the middle of December, I awoke, suddenly aware that some noise had fallen like a heavy stone into my dreams. As I felt for the matches it came again, the long, grudging groan and the uncompromising bang of the cross door at the head of the kitchen stairs. I told myself that it was a draught that had done it, but it was a perfectly still night. Even as I listened, a sound of wheels on the avenue shook the stillness. The thing was getting past a joke. In a few minutes I was stealthily groping my way down my own staircase, with a box of matches in my hand, enforced by scientific curiosity, but none the less armed with a stick. I stood in the dark at the top of the back stairs and listened; the snores of Mrs. Cadogan and her nephew Peter rose tranquilly from their respective lairs. I descended to the kitchen and lit a candle; there was nothing unusual. there, except a great portion of the Cadogan wearing apparel, which was arranged at the fire, and was being serenaded by two crickets. Whatever had opened the door, my household was blameless.

The kitchen was not attractive, yet I felt indisposed to leave it. None the less, it appeared to be my duty to inspect the yard. I put the candle on the table and went forth into the outer darkness. Not a sound was to be heard. The night was very cold, and so dark, that I could scarcely distinguish the roofs of the stables against the sky; the house loomed tall and oppressive above me; I was conscious of how lonely it stood in the dumb and barren country. Spirits were certainly futile creatures, childish in their manifestations, stupidly content with the old machinery of raps and rumbles. I thought how fine a scene might be played on a stage like this; if I were a ghost, how bluely I would glimmer at the windows, how whimperingly chatter in the wind. Something whirled out of the darkness above me, and fell with a flop on the ground, just at my feet. I jumped backwards, in point of fact I made for the kitchen door, and, with my hand on the latch, stood still and waited. Nothing further happened; the thing that lay there did not stir. I struck a match. The moment of tension turned to bathos as the light flickered on nothing more fateful than a dead crow.

Dead it certainly was. I could have told that without looking at it; but why should it, at some considerable period after its death, fall from the clouds at my feet. But did it fall from the clouds? I struck another match, and stared up at the impenetrable face of the house. There was no hint of solution in the dark windows, but I determined to go up and search the rooms that gave upon the yard.

How cold it was! I can feel now the frozen musty air of those attics, with their rat-eaten floors and wall papers furred with damp. I went softly from one to another, feeling like a burglar in my own house, and found nothing in elucidation of the mystery. The windows were hermetically shut, and sealed with cobwebs. There was no furniture, except in the end room, where a wardrobe without doors stood in a corner, empty save for the solemn presence of a monstrous tall hat. I went back to bed, cursing those powers of darkness that had got me out of it, and heard no more.

My landlord had not failed of his promise to visit my coverts with his hounds; in fact, he fulfilled it rather more conscientiously than seemed to me quite wholesome for the cock-shooting. I maintained a silence which I felt to be magnanimous on the part of a man who cared nothing for hunting and a great deal for shooting, and wished the hounds more success in the slaughter of my foxes than seemed to be granted to them. I met them all, one red frosty evening, as I drove down the long hill to my demesne gates, Flurry at their head, in his shabby pink coat and dingy breeches, the hounds trailing dejectedly behind him and his half-dozen companions.

MY FRIEND SLIPPER

'What luck?' I called out, drawing rein as I met them.

'None,' said Mr. Flurry briefly. He did not stop, neither did he remove his pipe from the down-twisted corner of his mouth; his eye at me was cold and sour. The other members of the hunt passed me with equal hauteur; I thought they took their ill luck very badly.

On foot, among the last of the straggling hounds, cracking a carman's whip, and swearing comprehensively at them all, slouched my friend Slipper. Our friendship had begun in Court, the relative positions of the dock and the judgment seat forming no obstacle to its progress, and had been cemented during several days' tramping after snipe. He was, as usual, a little drunk, and he hailed me as though I were a ship.

'Ahoy, Major Yeates!' he shouted, bringing himself up with a lurch against my cart; 'it's hunting ye should be, in place of sending poor divils to gaol!'

'But I hear you had no hunting,' I said.

'Ye heard that, did ye?' Slipper rolled upon me an eye like that of a profligate pug. 'Well, begor, ye heard no more than the thruth.'

'But where are all the foxes?' said I.

'Begor, I don't know no more than your honour. And Shreelane—that there used to be as many foxes in it as there's crosses in a yard of check! Well, well, I'll say nothin' for it, only that it's quare! Here, Vaynus! Naygress!' Slipper uttered a yell, hoarse with whisky, in adjuration of two elderly ladies of the pack who had profited by our conversation to stray away into an adjacent cottage. 'Well, good-night, Major. Mr. Flurry's as cross as briars, and he'll have me ate!'

He set off at a surprisingly steady run, cracking his whip, and whooping like a madman. I hope that when I also am sixty I shall be able to run like Slipper.

That frosty evening was followed by three others like unto it, and a flight of woodcock came in. I calculated that I could do with five guns, and I despatched invitations to shoot and dine on the following day to four of the local sportsmen, among whom was, of course, my landlord. I remember that in my letter to the latter I expressed a facetious hope that my bag of cock would be more successful than his of foxes had been.

The answers to my invitations were not what I expected. All, without so much as a conventional regret, declined my invitation; Mr. Knox added that he hoped the bag of cock would be to my liking, and that I need not be 'affraid' that the hounds would trouble my coverts any more. Here was war! I gazed in stupefaction at the crooked scrawl in which my landlord had declared it. It was wholly and entirely inexplicable, and instead of going to sleep comfortably over the fire and my newspaper as a gentleman should, I spent the evening in irritated ponderings over this bewildering and exasperating change of front on the part of my friendly squireens.

My shoot the next day was scarcely a success. I shot the woods in company with my gamekeeper, Tim Connor, a gentleman whose duties mainly consisted in limiting the poaching privileges to his personal friends, and whatever my offence might have been, Mr. Knox could have wished me no bitterer punishment than hearing the unavailing shouts of 'Mark Cock!' and seeing my birds winging their way from the coverts, far out of shot. Tim Connor and I got ten couple between us; it might have been thirty if my neighbours had not boycotted me, for what I could only suppose was the slackness of their hounds.

I was dog-tired that night, having walked enough for three men, and I slept the deep, insatiable sleep that I had earned. It was somewhere about 3 A.M. that I was gradually awakened by a continuous knocking, interspersed with muffled calls. Great-Uncle McCarthy had never before given tongue, and I freed one ear from blankets to listen. Then I remembered that Peter had told me the sweep had promised to arrive that morning, and to arrive early. Blind with sleep and fury I went to the passage window, and thence desired the sweep to go to the devil. It availed me little. For the remainder of the night I could hear him pacing round the house, trying the windows, banging at the doors, and calling upon Peter Cadogan as the priests of Baal called upon their god. At 6 o'clock I had fallen into a troubled doze, when Mrs. Cadogan knocked at my door and imparted the information that the sweep had arrived. My answer need not be recorded, but in spite of it the door opened, and my housekeeper, in a weird *déshabille*, effectively lighted by the orange beams of her candle, entered my room.

'God forgive me, I never seen one I'd hate as much as that sweep !' she began ; 'he's these three hours—arrah, what, three hours !—no, but all night, raising tallywack and tandem round the house to get at the chimbleys.'

'Well, for heaven's sake let him get at the chimneys and let me go to sleep,' I answered, goaded to desperation, 'and you may tell him from me that if I hear his voice again I'll shoot him !'

Mrs. Cadogan silently left my bedside, and as she closed the door she said to herself, 'The Lord save us !'

Subsequent events may be briefly summarised. At 7.30 I was wakened anew by a thunderous sound in the chimney, and a brick crashed into the fireplace, followed at a short interval by two dead jackdaws and their nests. At 8, I was informed by Peter that there was no hot water, and that he wished the divil would roast the same sweep. At 9.30, when I came down to breakfast, there was no fire anywhere, and my coffee, made in the coach-house, tasted of soot. I put on an overcoat and opened my letters. About fourth or fifth in the uninteresting heap came one in an egregiously disguised hand.

'Sir,' it began, 'this is to inform you your unsportsmanlike conduct has been discovered. You have been suspected this good while of shooting the Shreelane foxes, it is known now you do worse. Parties have seen your gamekeeper going regular to meet the Saturday early train at Salters Hill Station, with your grey horse under a cart, and your labels on the boxes, and we know as well as *your agent in Cork* what it is you have in those boxes. Be warned in time.—Your Wellwisher.'

I read this through twice before its drift became apparent, and I realised that I was accused of improving my shooting and my finances by the simple expedient of selling my foxes. That is to say, I was in a worse position than if I had stolen a horse, or murdered Mrs. Cadogan, or got drunk three times a week in Skebawn.

For a few moments I fell into wild laughter, and then, aware that it was rather a bad business to let a lie of this kind get a start, I sat down to demolish the preposterous charge in a letter to Flurry Knox. Somehow, as I selected my sentences, it was borne in upon me that, if the letter spoke the truth, circumstantial evidence was rather against me. Mere lofty repudiation would be unavailing, and by my infernal facetiousness about the woodcock I had effectively filled in the case against myself. At all events, the first thing to do was to establish a basis, and have it out with Tim Connor. I rang the bell.

' Peter, is Tim Connor about the place? '

' He is not, sir. I heard him say he was going west the hill to mend the bounds fence.' Peter's face was covered with soot, his eyes were red, and he coughed ostentatiously. ' The sweep's after breaking one of his brushes within in yer bedroom chimney, sir,' he went on, with all the satisfaction of his class in announcing domestic calamity ; ' he's above on the roof now, and he'd be thankful to you to go up to him.'

I followed him upstairs in that state of simmering patience that any employer of Irish labour must know and sympathise with. I climbed the rickety ladder and squeezed through the dirty trapdoor involved in the ascent to the roof, and was confronted by the hideous face of the sweep, black against the frosty blue sky. He had encamped with all his paraphernalia on the flat top of the roof, and was good enough to rise and put his pipe in his pocket on my arrival.

' Good morning, Major. That's a grand view you have up here,' said the sweep. He was evidently far too well-bred to talk shop. ' I thravelled every roof in this counthry, and there isn't one where you'd get as handsome a prospect ! '

Theoretically he was right, but I had not come up to the roof to discuss scenery, and demanded brutally why he had sent for me. The explanation involved a recital of the special genius required to sweep the Shreelane chimneys; of the fact that the sweep had in infancy been sent up and down every one of them by Great-Uncle McCarthy; of the three ass-loads of soot that by his peculiar skill he had this morning taken from the kitchen chimney; of its present purity, the draught being such that it would ' dhraw up a young cat with it.' Finally—realising that I could endure no more—he explained that my bedroom chimney had got what he called ' a wynd' in it, and he proposed to climb down a little way in the stack to try 'would he get to come at the brush.' The sweep was very small, the chimney very large. I stipulated that he should have a rope round his waist, and despite the illegality, I let him go. He went down like a monkey, digging his toes and fingers into the niches made for the purpose in the old chimney; Peter held the rope. I lit a cigarette and waited.

Certainly the view from the roof was worth coming up to look at. It was rough, heathery country on one side, with a string of little blue lakes running like a turquoise necklet round the base of a firry hill, and patches of pale green pasture were set amidst the rocks and heather. A silvery flash behind the undulations of the hills told where the Atlantic lay in immense plains of sunlight. I turned to survey with an owner's eye my own grey woods and straggling plantations of larch, and espied a man coming out of the western wood. He had something on his back, and he was walking very fast; a rabbit poacher no doubt. As he passed out of sight into the back avenue. I saw he was beginning to run. At the same instant I saw on the hill beyond my western boundaries half a dozen horsemen scrambling by zigzag ways down towards the wood. There was one red coat among them; it came first at the gap in the fence that Tim Connor had gone out to mend, and with the others was lost to sight in the covert, from which, in another instant, came clearly through the frosty air a shout of ' Gone to ground ! ' Tremendous horn blowings followed, then, all in the same moment, I saw the hounds break in full cry from the wood, and come stringing over the grass and up the back avenue towards the yard gate. Were they running a fresh fox into the stables?

I do not profess to be a hunting-man, but I am an Irishman, and so, it is perhaps superfluous to state, is Peter. We forgot the sweep as if he had never existed, and precipitated ourselves down the ladder, down the stairs, and out into the yard. One side of the yard is formed by the coach-house and a long stable, with a range of lofts above them, planned on the heroic scale in such matters that obtained in Ireland formerly. These join the house at the corner by the back door. A long flight of stone steps leads to the lofts, and up these, as Peter and I emerged from the back door, the hounds were struggling helter-skelter. Almost simultaneously there was a confused clatter of hoofs in the back avenue, and Flurry Knox came stooping at a gallop under the archway followed by three or four other riders. They flung themselves from their horses and made for the steps of the loft; more hounds pressed, yelling, on their heels, the din was indescribable, and justified Mrs. Cadogan's subsequent remark that ' when she heard the noise she thought the divil and all his young ones was broke loose.'

I jostled in the wake of the party, and found myself in the loft, wading in hay, and nearly deafened by the clamour that was bandied about the high roof and walls. At the further end of the loft the hounds were raging in the hay, encouraged thereto by the whoops and screeches of Flurry and his friends. High up in the gable of the loft, where it joined the main wall of the house, there was a small door, and I noted with a transient surprise that there was a long ladder leading up to it. Even as it caught my eye a hound fought his way out of a drift of hay and began to jump at the ladder, throwing his tongue vociferously, and even clambering up a few rungs in his excitement.

' There's the way he's gone ! ' roared Flurry, striving through hounds and hay towards the ladder, ' Trumpeter has him ! What's up there, back of the door, Major ? I don't remember it at all.'

My crimes had evidently been forgotten in the supremacy of the moment. While I was futilely asserting that had the fox gone up the ladder he could not possibly have opened the door and shut it after him, even if the door led anywhere, which, to the best of my belief, it did not, the door in question opened, and to my amazement the sweep appeared at it. He gesticulated violently, and over the tumult was heard to asseverate that there was nothing above there, only a way into the flue, and anyone would be destroyed with the soot——

' Ah, go to blazes with your soot ! ' interrupted Flurry, already half-way up the ladder.

I followed him, the other men pressing up behind me. That Trumpeter had made no mistake was instantly brought home to our noses by the reek of fox that met us at the door. Instead of a chimney, we found ourselves in a dilapidated bedroom, full of people. Tim Connor was there, the sweep was there, and a

THE SWEEP WAS HEARD TO ASSEVERATE THERE WAS NOTHING ABOVE THERE,
ONLY A WAY INTO THE FLUE

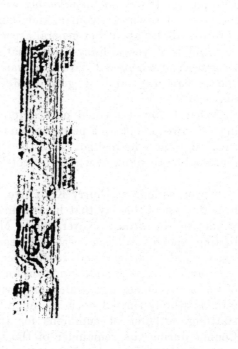

squalid elderly man and woman on whom I had never set eyes before. There was a large open fireplace, black with the soot the sweep had brought down with him, and on the table stood a bottle of my own special Scotch whisky. In one corner of the room was a pile of broken packing cases, and beside these on the floor lay a bag in which something kicked.

Flurry, looking more uncomfortable and nonplussed than I could have believed possible, listened in silence to the ceaseless harangue of the elderly woman. The hounds were yelling like lost spirits in the loft below, but her voice pierced the uproar like a bagpipe. It was an unspeakably vulgar voice, yet it was not the voice of a countrywoman, and there were frowzy remnants of respectability about her general aspect.

'And is it you, Flurry Knox, that's calling me a disgrace! Disgrace, indeed, am I? Me that was your poor mother's own uncle's daughter, and as good a McCarthy as ever stood in Shreelane!'

What followed I could not comprehend, owing to the fact that the sweep kept up a perpetual under-current of explanation to me as to how he had got down the wrong chimney. I noticed that his breath stank of whisky—Scotch, not the native variety.

.   .   .   .   .   .

Never, as long as Flurry Knox lives to blow a horn, will he hear the last of the day that he ran his mother's first cousin to ground in the attic. Never, while Mrs. Cadogan can hold a basting spoon, will she cease to recount how, on the same occasion, she plucked and roasted ten couple of woodcock in one torrid hour to provide luncheon for the hunt. In the glory of this achievement her confederacy with the stowaways in the attic is wholly slurred over, in much the same manner as the startling outburst of summons for trespass, brought by Tim Connor during the remainder of the shooting season, obscured the unfortunate episode of the bagged fox. It was, of course, zeal for my shooting that induced him to assist Mr. Knox's disreputable relations in the deportation of my foxes; and I have allowed it to remain at that.

In fact, the only things not allowed to remain were Mr. and Mrs. McCarthy Gannon. They, as my landlord informed me, in the midst of vast apologies, had been permitted to squat at Shreelane until my tenancy began, and having then ostentatiously and abusively left the house, they had, with the connivance of the Cadogans, secretly returned to roost in the corner attic, to sell foxes under the ægis of my name, and to make inroads on my belongings.   They retained connection with the outer world by means of the ladder and the loft, and with the house in general, and my whisky in particular, by a door into the other attics — a door concealed by the wardrobe in which reposed Great-Uncle McCarthy's tall hat.

It is with the greatest regret that I relinquish the prospect of writing a monograph on Great-Uncle McCarthy for a Spiritualistic Journal, but with the departure of his relations he ceased to manifest himself, and neither the nailing up of packing cases, nor the rumble of the cart that took them to the station, disturbed my sleep for the future.

I understand that the task of clearing out the McCarthy Gannon's effects was of a nature that necessitated two glasses of whisky per man ; and if the remnants of rabbit and jackdaw disinterred in the process were anything like the crow that was thrown out of the window at my feet, I do not grudge the restorative.

As Mrs. Cadogan remarked to the sweep, 'A Turk couldn't stand it.'

CPSIA information can be obtained
at www.ICGtesting.com
Printed in the USA
LVOW13*0535120218
566112LV00010BA/93/P